This kangaroo belongs to:

. . . .

To all the people who support and protect
kangaroos and other Australian animals – G. D.

To Aneisha Quelle Maglalang – A. B.

This book contains some Aussie words you might not be
familiar with. This is what they mean:

    billabong: a pool of water left behind after
    a flood or when a river changes direction
    (from the Wiradjuri word *bilabang*).
    cricket: a bat-and-ball sport played between
    two teams.
    googly: a special trick when playing cricket.
    The bowler spins the ball one way but makes it
    look like it will spin the other way.

If I had a kangaroo © 2022 Thames & Hudson Ltd, London
Text © 2022 Gabby Dawnay
Illustrations © 2022 Alex Barrow

First published in 2022 in the United States of America by
Thames & Hudson Inc., 500 Fifth Avenue, New York,
New York 10110

Library of Congress Control Number 2021943318

ISBN 978-0-500-65268-8

Printed and bound in China by Everbest Printing Co. Ltd

Be the first to know about our new releases,
exclusive content and author events by visiting
thamesandhudson.com
thamesandhudsonusa.com
thamesandhudson.com.au

GABBY DAWNAY
ALEX BARROW

If I had a
kangaroo

T&H

I do like bats,

I'm scared of snakes,

A platypus? Too shy!

I wouldn't mind an emu
(even though they cannot fly...)

A roly-poly wombat?

Or a koala that could cling?

No, I prefer the kind of pet
that has a bit of SPRING!

I really want a BOUNCY pet,
to hop around and play.
We'd BOING along the billabong
and always shout "G'day!"

Oh if I had a **KANGA**...

ROO

she'd carry me around.
We'd get to places extra quick
with one enormous bound!

If I had a kangaroo
I'd keep her fit and trim
by jumping on the trampoline
each day inside the gym!

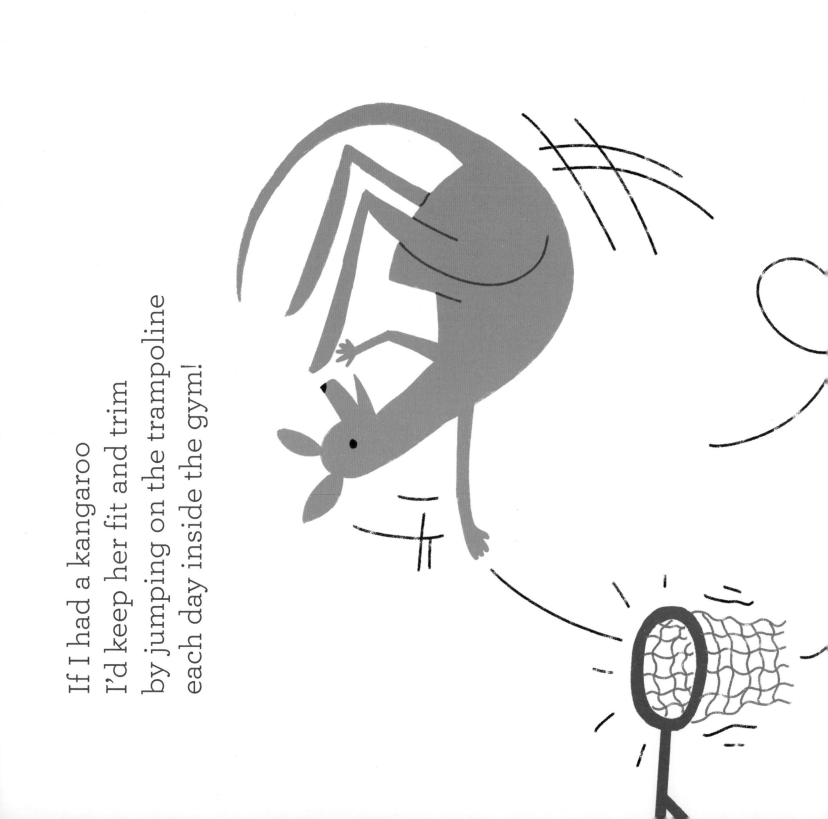

My kangaroo could mow the lawn,
it wouldn't take her long...

For kangaroos are herbivores
and veggies make them strong!

If I had a kangaroo
I'd have to take her shopping,
so she could help me choose new shoes—
the very best for hopping!

Kangaroos are good at sports,
so in a cricket match
she'd bowl a spinning googly...

And she'd use her pouch to catch!

My kangaroo would carry
and deliver all the mail...
Then after she had finished,
take a rest upon her tail!

Whatever kind of weather,
how my kangaroo would prance...

In sunshine, rain or hurricane
there's always time to dance!

My kangaroo would barbecue
and I would use a scoop
to clear away the garbage—
or perhaps a kanga...

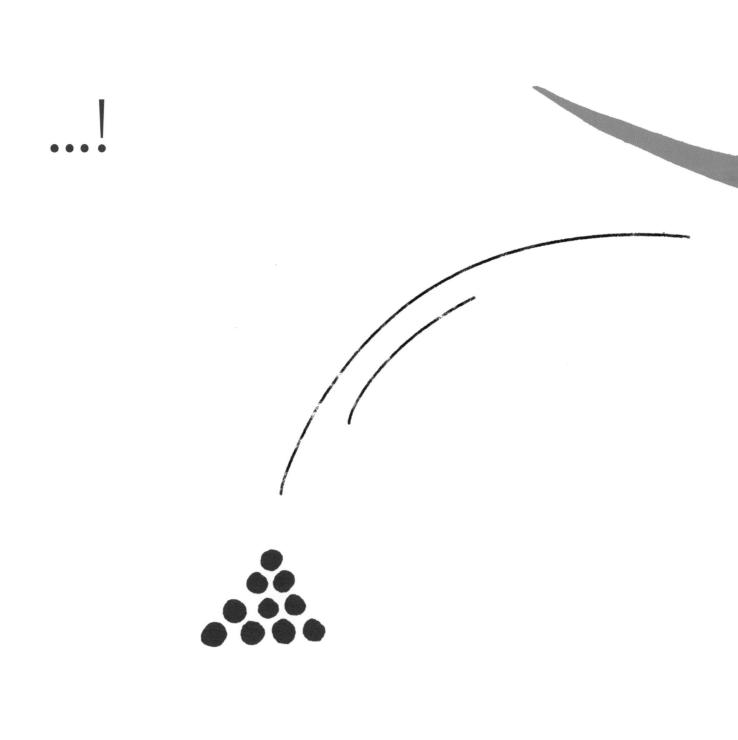

If I had a kangaroo
imagine all the tricks...
she'd fill the bath with bubbles
from her super-turbo-kicks!

We'd read a bedtime story
while snuggled on the couch.

And then, when it was bedtime
I would jump inside her pouch!

If I had a kangaroo
the places we'd explore—
from red and dusty deserts
to the turquoise ocean shore...

From beaches to the mountains,
all the animals we'd see...
Imagine the adventures
for my kangaroo and me!

Discover more exciting
animals in the series...